# The Mean Monkey

by Rachel DelaHaye
illustrated by Julian Mosedale

CAMBRIDGE
UNIVERSITY PRESS

Institute of Education

Babbo sat in a coconut tree.

'Look at me!' he said to Kamal.

'Look at me, up here in the tree.'

Kamal looked up.

'That looks like a good tree,' said Kamal.

'I can see lots of coconuts to eat.'

'Oh no!' said Babbo. 'All the coconuts are for me.'

Kamal looked up at Babbo.

'Don't be mean, Babbo,' he said.

'I can come up and help you pick the coconuts.'

'This is my tree,' said Babbo.

'**I** will eat all the coconuts.'

5

Kamal began to climb up the tree.

But Babbo jumped up and down.

He picked a coconut

and threw it at Kamal.

Kamal went to tell all the monkeys.

'Babbo is a mean monkey,' he said.

'He wants to eat all the coconuts.'

They made a plan.

Babbo looked at all the coconuts.

Babbo looked at the monkeys.

'They will come
and take my coconuts,'
he said to himself.

'One, two, three, go!' shouted Kamal.

The monkeys started to climb the tree.

'Get away!' Babbo shouted.

'Get away from my tree!'

But the monkeys kept on climbing.

11

Babbo looked at the coconuts.

He started to throw them at the monkeys.

'Look out!' Kamal shouted
to the monkeys.

The coconuts did not hit them.
But Babbo went on throwing.

Kamal looked at the coconuts on the ground.

He looked at the monkeys in the tree.

'You can come down now,' he said.

14

'Go away,' said Babbo.
'The coconuts in the tree are all for me.'

'Yes,' smiled Kamal. '**They** are all for you.'

# The Mean Monkey  Rachel DelaHaye

Teaching notes written by Glen Franklin and Sue Bodman

## Using this book

### Developing reading comprehension

Babbo has found a tree full of coconuts and he doesn't want to share them. Even Kamal's offer of help to pick the coconuts doesn't shift Babbo from his mean attitude. Kamal's cunning plan results in a much fairer approach to sharing the coconuts – but does Babbo realise that he has been tricked? Attending to punctuation is key to gaining the full meaning of the text and reading with appropriate expression.

### Grammar and sentence structure

- Speech punctuation indicates the different characters speaking, such as the conversation between Babbo and Kamal on p.3.
- Sentence lengths vary to create effect, for example using short sentences in dialogue: *'Look at me'* on p.2, *'This is my tree'* on p.5.

### Word meaning and spelling

- Multi syllabic words (*'himself'*, *'coconut'*) can be read by identifying parts of words.
- Opportunity to rehearse automatic, fast recognition of high-frequency words.

### Curriculum links

*Science and Nature* – Monkeys are primarily leaf eaters, but most are omnivores. Children could use the Internet and non-fiction texts to explore what monkeys living in different habitats eat.

*Literacy* – Babbo has behaved badly. The children could write a letter from Babbo to the monkeys, apologising for being mean and promising to share the coconuts in the future.

## Learning Outcomes

Children can:

- monitor their own errors and show a greater degree of independent self-correction reread to check meaning is conveyed through phrasing and expression
- discuss the story to demonstrate understanding.

## A guided reading lesson

### Book Introduction

Ask the children if they know what it is to be mean. *Has anyone ever been mean to you? Maybe they wouldn't play, or maybe they were unkind.* Give each child a copy of the book. Read the title and the blurb with them. Draw the children's attention to Babbo clutching the coconuts, with a mean expression on his face.

### Orientation

Give a brief overview of the story, using the same verb tense as used in the book. Say: *In this story, Babbo the monkey is mean. He won't share the coconuts with the other monkeys, even though he can't eat all those by himself. Let's read what happens.*

### Preparation

Page 2 and 3: Discuss how Babbo calls out to Kamal to show off about how many coconuts he has and that it is a *'good tree'*. Draw attention to the word *'coconut'* so that the children have a strategy for reading it throughout the book. Say: *It's a coconut tree. Listen to the parts of the word co-co-nut. Find that word on the page. Look at the parts of the word. Now put them all together and read the word a few times.*

Page 3: Explore the conversation and speech punctuation on this page. An exclamation mark doesn't always mean shouting or